The Lion and the Mouse

Based on a story by Aesop

Retold by Mairi Mackinnon
Illustrated by Frank Endersby

Reading Consultant: Alison Kelly
Roehampton University

Lion was fast asleep.

2

Something tickled
his nose.

Aaaaaa-choooooooooooo!!!

Lion woke up.

5

A mouse!

"How dare you wake
me!" Lion roared.

He raised his paw...

8

"Please don't kill me,"
begged the mouse.

"Maybe I can save
your life too, one day."

Lion laughed.

You're too small to save anyone!

The next day, Lion
walked into a trap.

The mouse heard him.

16

She nibbled through
the ropes...

...and Lion was free.

"I'm sorry, little mouse," said Lion.

"I was wrong. Even little friends can be good friends."

PUZZLES

Puzzle 1

Can you put the pictures
in the right order?

A

"Ha ha ha!"

B

"Don't kill me!"

C

Tickle, tickle…

D

"Aaa-chooo!"

E

"Zzzzz"

Puzzle 2

Choose three good words to describe Lion, and three to describe Mouse.

big green jumping helpless

scared slimy golden small

smiling lazy fierce sleeping

Puzzle 3

Choose the best sentence
for each picture.

A

Lion is awake.
Lion is asleep.

B

Mouse is scared.
Mouse is scary.

C

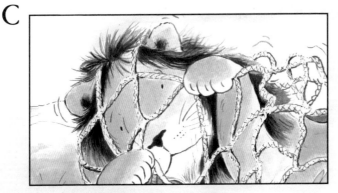

Lion is tired.
Lion is trapped.

D

Lion is silly.
Lion is sorry.

Answers to puzzles

Puzzle 1

E

"Zzzzz"

C

Tickle, tickle...

D

"Aaa-chooo!"

B

"Don't kill me!"

A

"Ha ha ha!"

Puzzle 2

Lion: big, fierce, golden

Mouse: small, scared, helpless

Puzzle 3

A

Lion is asleep.

B

Mouse is scared.

C

Lion is trapped.

D

Lion is sorry.

About the story

The Lion and the Mouse is one of Aesop's Fables, a collection of stories first told in Ancient Greece around 4,000 years ago. The stories always have a "moral" (a message or lesson) at the end.

Designed by Michelle Lawrence
Series designer: Russell Punter
Series editor: Lesley Sims

First published in 2008 by Usborne Publishing Ltd., Usborne House,
83-85 Saffron Hill, London EC1N 8RT, England. www.usborne.com
Copyright © 2008 Usborne Publishing Ltd.